*The Boxcar Children Mysteries*

# THE PIZZA MYSTERY

### created by
## GERTRUDE CHANDLER WARNER

*Illustrated by Charles Tang*

**ALBERT WHITMAN & Company**
Morton Grove, Illinois

ISBN 0-8075-6535-0

1 3 5 7 9 10 8 6 4 2

Printed in the U.S.A.

# Contents

# CHAPTER 1

## *Not Hungry*

Four children and one dog were sound asleep in the roomy black car. James Alden, the children's grandfather, took one hand off the steering wheel. He patted Benny Alden's curly head, but the six-year-old boy didn't stir.

In the rearview mirror, Mr. Alden checked on his three older grandchildren. Henry, Jessie, and Violet looked like sleepy puppies in the back seat. The Aldens had been on the road for hours. Still, the long drive home to Greenfield was only half over.

"It's not often my copilots are so quiet," Mr. Alden chuckled to himself.

None of the children moved. Their dog, Watch, thumped his tail just once from under the dashboard. Then he went right on snoozing, too. Everyone in the warm, cozy car was tired after a weekend of skating, tobogganing, and hiking in the snow up north.

"Not nearly as much snow around Silver Falls," Mr. Alden said to no one in particular.

"Silver Falls?" Benny mumbled. He didn't open his eyes.

"That's right, Benny," Mr. Alden said. "Just a few more miles to Silver Falls."

Suddenly Benny sat straight up. He looked out the car window. "Hey, Grandfather, you're right! We just passed Aunt Millie's Fudge House. If I weren't saving room for Mr. and Mrs. Piccolo's Pizza in Silver Falls, I'd hop out of the car right now for some of that fudge."

"Fudge!" Jessie cried when she overheard Benny. "Before lunch?"

"Maybe just a skinny piece," Benny told his big sister.

Now that Benny was up, he wanted everyone else up, too. "Come on, Watch. Go wake Henry, boy."

Watch knew very well that his dog nap was over. He yawned a wide, toothy yawn then shook himself awake.

"Whoa, boy, whoa," fourteen-year-old Henry said when he felt Watch step all over him. He yawned a big yawn, too. He had been up since five-thirty that morning. Packing the car with the Aldens' snowshoes, cross-country skis, and toboggan had taken him and Jessie a long time. Not that they minded. Like all the Aldens, they enjoyed hard work.

Only ten-year-old Violet was still napping. Watch gave Violet a lick on the cheek, and her long brown lashes fluttered open.

"That tickles," Violet said when she woke up with a sweet, dreamy smile.

"Entering Silver Falls," twelve-year-old Jessie announced. She smoothed her long brown hair. Then she gathered up the books and games scattered across the backseat. She found a lumpy toy bear. "Here's Stockings, Benny. He was squeezed between the seats."

Benny reached back and gave his favorite old bear a hug. He had many new toys since Grandfather Alden had adopted the children after their parents died. But Stockings was special. Jessie had made the cloth bear out of Benny's old socks back in the days when the children were living in a boxcar in the woods all by themselves. Now, just like the children, Stockings had a comfortable home with Mr. Alden, too.

Violet gathered up her box of art supplies and work bag now that they were getting near Silver Falls. "May we stop at Tom's Gas Station, Grandfather?" Violet asked. "We always do."

"Indeed we do!" Mr. Alden slowed down. "Why, Tom Morgan would never forgive us if we didn't stop by to fill up on gas."

"Or bubble gum!" Benny cried out. He jiggled a pocket full of change. "I saved twelve pennies for that old gumball machine. That's twelve chances to win one of the foil-covered gumballs and get a free treat."

Benny Alden was lucky in most things, but not when it came to winning silver gumballs. The Aldens had stopped at Tom's Gas Station on many family trips. In all those times Benny had never won a prize foil-covered gumball. Today that was going to change!

Jessie spotted the small brick station first. "Good old Tom's," she said in a happy voice.

Mr. Alden pulled up close to the gas pumps. He knew his grandchildren liked to talk to Tom while he checked the car.

"Howdy do, folks," Tom said when he came over to the car. "I'd know this wonderful car of yours anywhere, Mr. Alden. Still going tip-top, I see. Never met anybody who kept a classic like this in such good shape. Fill 'er up?"

"Sure thing." Grandfather got out of the car to stretch his legs and take Watch for a quick walk.

The Aldens liked to watch Tom Morgan work. When he filled the tank the bill always came out exactly on the dollar, not a penny

over or a penny under. With Henry and Benny's help, Tom got the windows and headlights shining again.

The children looked on as Tom checked under the hood.

"Now tell me about your latest adventure, Benny," Tom asked. "Did you solve any mysteries up north? Or catch any crooks?"

"Naw." Benny sounded disappointed. "Nothing happened. I found an old newspaper stuffed into a windowsill, but it was only to keep out the cold. One night a noise at the window woke us up. But it was only an icy branch scraping against the cabin."

"Well, your trip's not over yet," Tom said with a smile. "Here, Jessie, let's see if you still remember how to check the oil."

Jessie slid the dipstick down into the oil tank. She brought it back up smoothly. "Still plenty of oil, Tom."

When they had finished with the car, the Aldens headed inside the little store Tom ran as part of the gas station. One by one, Benny dropped most of his pennies into the gumball machine. He twirled the crank as fast as he could.

"Phooey, phooey!" the other Aldens heard Benny complain as one ordinary gumball after another rolled out.

"I've only got five pennies left," Benny said, making a face at the machine. "I'm going to give this old machine a rest for a minute. I better think about Piccolos' Pizza so I don't get any madder."

The Aldens all laughed. Violet was the first one to notice that Tom wasn't laughing along with them. Instead, he gave Benny some extra pennies someone had left on the counter.

"Here, Benny," he said in a quiet voice. "Maybe this will help you. I'm not so sure how things will be when you stop at Piccolos' Pizza."

Jessie stared at Tom. Her big brown eyes were full of questions. "What is it, Tom? Is something the matter with Mr. and Mrs. Piccolo?"

Tom looked sad and puzzled. "The Piccolos are having a hard time keeping the restaurant going," he said. "Nobody can figure out why. For the last couple of months they've been keeping very irregular hours. Sometimes they're not open at — "

Before Tom could finish, everyone heard a loud car horn honking. Watch pulled on his leash and barked. Tom dropped the Aldens' money on the counter without even ringing up their bill. He walked out to the big, fancy car that was making all the noise.

"Quiet, Watch, quiet," Jessie said. Even when he didn't want to, Watch always obeyed Jessie. He lowered his bark to a growl.

Outside, a tall, annoyed-looking man got out of the car. He stood over Tom and shouted orders. The Aldens could hear every loud word from inside the station. "Check the oil! Then the water. And don't forget the windows!"

Benny took his last few pennies. Slowly, he put one after the other into the gumball machine. He was just about to turn the crank after the last penny, when the man burst into the station.

"Is there a soda machine in this place?" he shouted as if the Aldens were supposed to serve him.

Without waiting for an answer, the man shoved some coins into the soda machine. He popped the top off the can. After a couple of big gulps, he left the half-full can on a shelf.

At the counter, the man shifted from one foot to the other. "What's that dog doing in here?" he asked when Watch growled at him.

Henry tugged on Watch's leash and took him outside. Even that didn't stop Watch from growling.

"Come, children," Mr. Alden said. "Let's get going to Piccolos'. The sooner we get there, the sooner we get some of that good pizza we came for."

"Don't count on it!" the man spat out. "You'll be lucky if it's even open!"

Before the Aldens could try to figure this out, Tom came back into the station. "All set, Mr. Irons. Let me get these folks on the road, then I'll write up your charge."

"I'm in a hurry," the man snapped. He slapped down a pile of bills on the counter.

"Oh, and take out money for a pack of gum."

"What kind would you like, Mr. Irons?" Tom asked.

The man didn't bother to answer Tom's question. "Forget it." He reached into the pocket of his long black overcoat for a coin, then stuck it in the gumball machine.

"Wait! I still have a penny in there," Benny cried. It was too late.

The man turned the crank, and a silver gumball rolled out.

"Ha! My lucky day!" the man said with a rude laugh. "I guess you owe *me* that pack of gum for free. Make it spearmint."

Tom wasn't about to jump at these orders. "Sorry, but that was this boy's ball. If he said he had a penny in there, I'm sure he did. It's his prize."

The man pushed the door open and shouted on the way out, "Never mind. I hardly need a free prize."

Everyone heard the man's fancy car roar out of the station. The big car barely missed Tom's red tow truck.

"Who was that, Tom?" Grandfather asked.

"That's the new manager of the Mighty Mufflers factory," Tom said. "He's been running things while the owner, Mrs. Sturgis, is traveling on business. Problem is, he seems to think he can run things here, too, just because the company set up a charge account at my station. I'd almost rather not have the account."

Tom turned to Benny and handed him the prize silver gumball. "Hey, I know this is yours. Why don't you trade it in for a treat?"

Benny's lower lip trembled. "No, thanks," he said in a small voice. "I'm not hungry."

CHAPTER 2

## A Face at the Window

Benny pressed his nose against the cold, foggy window of the car. Half the fun of Silver Falls was a visit to Tom's Gas Station. But not that day.

Violet felt sorry for Benny. Then she thought of something. She drew a silly snowman on the misty window in the back. "Turn around, Benny. Look. Now you make one."

In no time, Benny had drawn a funny snowman on his window, too. When he had finished, he saw that Grandfather Alden was driving through the cheerful streets of Silver

Falls. It was lunchtime, and people were running errands or looking for a place to eat. "Is this the turn for Piccolos' Pizza, Grandfather?" Benny asked hopefully.

"Sure is," Mr. Alden answered. "Here's something Tom told me to give you."

Mr. Alden reached into his jacket pocket. He pulled out a package of Benny's favorite cookies.

"I'll save them for after lunch," Benny said when he saw the treat. "Look, Tom stuck a note on top. *For Benny, who had the winning penny.*"

"I guess you have to put up with all kinds when you own a gas station," Henry said. "That man should be glad to have a good mechanic like Tom to take care of his car, and he shouldn't get so sore about things."

Jessie felt the same way. "He even got mad about pizza!"

Benny turned around. "Not me! I'm *glad* about pizza. Are we there yet?"

Mr. Alden was confused. "Hmm. I thought we were, Benny, but I don't see the big Piccolos' Pizza sign."

The children twisted their heads every which way. Where was that nice, old pizza sign anyway?

The car passed a tall, new building that filled up the block. The Aldens couldn't find the pizza sign anywhere. Worse, they couldn't find Piccolos' Pizza, either!

Henry scratched his head. "We're on the right street, but everything looks different."

"And bigger," Violet said after they passed a giant parking lot filled with cars and trucks.

"Hey!" Benny yelled. "Look at that!" He pointed to a huge billboard showing a red car with a long silvery tailpipe. Underneath were the words: SILVER FALLS: HOME OF THE MIGHTY MUFFLERS.

Mr. Alden went around the block again. "That billboard covers the Piccolos' Pizza sign," he said. "We must have passed the restaurant by mistake."

Benny pressed his face against the window again. "I sure hope they didn't hide the restaurant behind that billboard too."

The second time around the block, everyone finally spotted the pizza place.

"No wonder we missed it," Henry cried, when Piccolos' Pizza came into view. "The new factory building practically blocks out the whole restaurant."

Mr. Alden drove slowly, searching for a parking place. "I can't imagine why Tom was worried. The restaurant must be crowded, what with all these cars. There's hardly an empty space."

"There's a space, Grandfather," Violet said. "Where that truck just pulled out."

Mr. Alden noticed a sign that said LOADING AREA — TRUCKS ONLY.

Jessie looked puzzled. "That doesn't make any sense. The Piccolos should have these parking spaces for their own customers."

"Well, I guess I'll have to squeeze in down the block," Mr. Alden said, and so he did just that.

It was a fairly long walk back to the restaurant. Along the way, the Aldens noticed how much the block had changed since their last visit to Silver Falls. This new factory stretched the whole length of the street, and so did the tall fence around the building.

"Not a very friendly-looking place the way the old factory was," Mr. Alden said.

"I sure wouldn't want to work here," Henry added. "Probably lots of customers for the Piccolos, though. Too bad the factory gate isn't closer. It is a long walk for pizza."

"Oh, no. Look!" Jessie said, stopping in the middle of the sidewalk. "There's that car again. At least I think it's the same car we saw at Tom's."

When the Aldens looked up, the same big car drove slowly past them.

Violet shivered. "It *is* that same awful man. Too bad he works right next door to the Piccolos. I hope he doesn't treat them the same way he treated Tom."

"I certainly hope not," Mr. Alden said.

The Aldens were in front of Piccolos' Pizza now. The two-story wooden building looked small and shabby squeezed up against the huge new factory. Although cars and trucks filled every space in front, the restaurant looked dim.

"Something is wrong here," Mr. Alden said in a worried voice.

"I know," Henry added. "Do you notice what's missing?"

"The pizza smell," Benny said in a quiet voice. "There's no pizza smell."

This was true. Here they were, right at the door. But the warm, delicious smell of pizza dough, all mixed together with cheese and tomato smells, wasn't in the air.

When Henry pushed open the creaky door, the little bell on top jingled. The Aldens stepped into the dim restaurant just as the twelve-thirty factory clock sounded. It was the middle of the lunch hour, but the Aldens' favorite pizza place was empty.

Violet pulled her jacket tighter. "It's chilly in here," she said.

Mr. Alden shivered too. "I wonder why the brick oven isn't going. Usually it's warm as toast in here."

Henry shook the door so the little bell would jingle again. "Maybe the Piccolos didn't hear us."

Finally, an old, white-haired man came out from the kitchen area in back. He looked at the Aldens as if they were strangers. The man almost seemed a stranger, too. But he wasn't. He was the Aldens' good friend, Mr. Piccolo, but he seemed much older.

"I'm sorry, but my oven isn't working today," the old man said. "But my wife and I can make you a sandwich or salad if you want."

Watch pulled away from Jessie and went up to the old man. The dog kept on wagging his tail eagerly until the old man noticed whose head he was patting.

"Oh, my!" the man cried. "It's Watch! And the Aldens! Oh, my, oh my! What a poor day it is when I don't recognize my old friends!"

Mr. Piccolo pulled his glasses from the pocket of his white apron. As soon as he put them on, his face lit up.

Mr. Alden put his hand out for a handshake. "Good to see you, Mr. Piccolo. Sorry we didn't call ahead from Tom's garage. We left there in a bit of confusion."

Mr. Piccolo pulled on one side of his bushy, white mustache. "No apologies, Mr. Alden. You know you and your family can

come here anytime." Then his voice dropped so low the Aldens could hardly hear him. "Well, I guess this is not the best time — no, not the best time at all. But here, sit down. I'll tell Nina you're here. She's trying to coax the little oven in the empty apartment upstairs to make a pizza."

Jessie ran out back and tied up Watch in the small back garden. Then she joined her family around their favorite table.

Benny looked around for the basket of crispy breadsticks. The Piccolos always kept them on the table for hungry customers. But there were no breadsticks to be seen. There was a stack of the red-and-white check tablecloths folded on the counter, but the tables were bare.

"I guess Tom was right about something being wrong," Violet whispered sadly. "There's no one here but the Piccolos. The tables aren't even set."

Henry shook his head. "Something doesn't add up. That big factory right next door — there must be hundreds of hungry workers in there. Why aren't they in here?"

"Ah," Mr. Piccolo answered, when he came back and overheard Henry's question. "I knew your family would see how things are. Today, well, today is another bad day. So many like this one. So many," he sighed. "This week it's the gas line to my oven not working. You know my oven. My father built that oven brick by brick when he came from Italy years ago. Not once did that oven quit. But now? No more gas in it. The builders digging at the factory, they cracked the gas line last week. You think we can make our pizza in a tiny apartment oven upstairs? No! No! No!"

"Yes! Yes! Yes!" Benny cried. "Hi, Mrs. Piccolo." He smiled at the woman who walked toward them with a tray of pizza.

She set the pizza in front of Benny. "For you," she said to Benny. After Henry cut the pizza into sections, Mrs. Piccolo frowned. "This pizza — it's not what you came for. But it's all we could manage with what I have. Go on. Take a bite."

The Aldens ate politely. None of them had the heart to tell the truth. This was not Piccolos' famous hot, crispy pizza. This pizza from the apartment oven upstairs was lukewarm and rubbery. Still, this didn't matter to the Aldens. Their dear friends had made this food, so they ate every bite.

Mr. Alden put down his napkin. "Tell us, why aren't you busy as all get out with that big new factory next door? Those workers must get hungry at lunch."

Mr. Piccolo pulled on his mustache and shook his head. "They are hungry, too hungry for our little place. At first they all came, full of good appetites."

Mrs. Piccolo fiddled with a thread on her apron. "Then someone put up that gate. It was too far away for people to walk to Piccolos'. When the factory got busier, the owners cut back the workers' lunch hours. No time for something like pizza. You know our pizza, it takes a long time. No rushing Piccolos' Pizza!"

Mr. Piccolo stood up and pointed out the front window. "You see all those delivery trucks from the factory? They took all my parking spaces away. Most of our old customers, they don't have a place to park now. They don't come so much. Then when Nick got sick and my other waiter left, well, we couldn't keep up."

Nick had worked for the Piccolos for many years, and the children were sad to hear he was sick. Especially Violet, who, on their trip through Silver Falls the year before, had helped Nick design new covers for the menus.

"Nick got sick?" Violet asked. "Will he be all right?"

Mr. Piccolo shrugged his shoulders. "We don't know. He moved out of the apartment upstairs, and after that he called in sick."

"He was like a son to us," Mrs. Piccolo said sadly. "And all of a sudden — he just picks up and leaves. And he won't tell us when he's coming back."

Mr. Piccolo began talking. "Things are so slow, maybe Nick, he doesn't want to come back."

The Aldens felt sad too. How everything had changed since their last visit! What could they do? How could they help? Even Benny didn't know what to say. He just stared out the window.

"Hey, who's that?" Benny cried out. He pointed to the small window that overlooked the kitchen area in back. "There's somebody looking inside the kitchen! Someone with a red hat."

Everyone looked up at the same time and saw a red blur. Henry and Jessie rushed out to the back garden where Watch was tied up. The dog was straining at his leash and panting.

"Look!" Jessie pointed to fresh footprints in the snow that led right to the window overlooking the kitchen. "Somebody *was* looking in."

"That's the other thing," Mr. Piccolo said when everyone calmed down. "This is not the first time we've seen someone outside, sneaking around the restaurant. I just don't know what's going on."

"Maybe it's time to retire," Mrs. Piccolo said sadly. "Just when we should be so busy."

The Aldens looked around the restaurant.

They remembered happier days and happier meals there.

Jessie said what the other Aldens were thinking. "We're on vacation for a couple of weeks. Maybe we can help you get busy again, at least until Nick returns."

"Maybe," Violet began, "if people can't come here, we can go to where they are!"

"That's a great idea!" Henry said. "I could fix up that old bike you used to keep in the shed out back, and once the oven's fixed, we could deliver pizzas right to your customers!"

"What do you think, Mr. Piccolo?" Grandfather asked. "Could my grandchildren give you a hand?"

"That would be wonderful!"

Grandfather stood up and headed for the door.

"Mr. Alden, Mr. Alden. Where are you going?" Mr. Piccolo asked.

Mr. Alden winked at the Piccolos. "Well, Watch and I are going home. That is, after my grandchildren unload their suitcases. I guess the rest of their vacation isn't going to be so quiet after all."

# CHAPTER 3

# Jessie's Pizza Plan

The apartment above Piccolos' Pizza wasn't empty for long. Mr. Alden and Watch left for Greenfield just as soon as the children got their luggage from the car. Grandfather promised to return in a couple of weeks. And they promised him a large Pizza Supreme when he came back.

Mr. Piccolo helped the children bring their belongings to the little apartment above the restaurant. "It will be good to hear footsteps overhead when I'm working," Mr.

Piccolo told the Aldens. "It's been too quiet since Nick moved out."

"I like this cozy apartment," Violet said when she looked around the sunlit rooms. "But I liked it better when Nick lived here."

"Remember all those wonderful stories he told us?" Benny asked.

"And the time he helped us build a snowman," Henry added.

"I miss Nick, too," Jessie said. "Where did he move?"

Mrs. Piccolo sighed. "He didn't tell us. He just left. Now that he's gone, I hope you children will fill these rooms with noise!"

"We will!" Benny yelled, and everyone laughed.

"Please get anything you want from the restaurant kitchen, anything at all," Mrs. Piccolo said.

After the Piccolos went to their own house a few blocks away, the children settled in. They dusted and scrubbed. They laid out their sleeping bags on the beds and the sofa. They covered the kitchen table with a cheery red-and-white tablecloth.

When they were finished, Henry put on his jacket. "I'm going to get the bike and take a ride over to the gas company. I know Mr. Piccolo said that someone from Mighty Mufflers called the gas company to get the broken line fixed. But what if they forgot? You know what Grandfather always says. Double check to make double sure."

"Well, come back hungry," Jessie told Henry as he zipped up his jacket. "Hungry for pizza!"

"I wouldn't count on it, Jessie," he said quietly. "Not today anyway. I don't think the gas company could fix the broken gas line so fast. But I'll do my best."

"And I'll do mine," Jessie said. She gave her brother a big smile. She had a plan, and when Jessie Alden had a plan, nothing could stop her.

"All this talk about pizza makes me hungry," Benny said. "I didn't eat very much before. The pizza just wasn't the same."

Jessie didn't seem to hear Benny. She was staring at the small electric stove in the kitchen. She was thinking about pizza, too.

"Violet," she said, "you and Benny go downstairs. Mrs. Piccolo said we could help ourselves to anything. Bring up two bags of pizza dough, some of her homemade sauce, and two blocks of mozzarella cheese. Then come right back up."

Violet and Bennie got going, but they weren't too hopeful. They knew that the Piccolos' big, hot brick oven was one of the secrets of their delicious pizza. The small apartment stove was good only for boiling eggs or making hot chocolate, not crispy pizza.

But Jessie had thoughts of her own. She turned the oven dial. "There. Four hundred degrees should be hot enough."

By the time Benny and Violet came back with all the pizza fixings, Jessie had new jobs for both of them. First she showed Violet how to work cornmeal into Mrs. Piccolo's dough. This would help it get crispy, even if it was baked in a small oven. Then she got Benny busy grating the soft mozzarella cheese into small piles. He gave Jessie a hungry look.

"Okay, okay, Benny. Save a small pile of cheese for yourself," Jessie told him. "Save the rest for our pizzas, all right?"

"Oh, goody!" Benny cried. "You just said 'pizzas' not 'pizza.' I could eat two big ones all by myself."

Jessie broke into a big smile. "Guess what, Benny? You might get to eat three or four pizzas! But not big ones — small ones. I figured out that the only thing wrong with the pizza Mrs. Piccolo made was that it was too big to bake in this oven."

Violet's face lit up, too. "I get it! Small pizzas for a small oven. Then they should get hot and crispy enough! I guess the Piccolos have been too upset to think of that."

In no time, the children had set up an assembly line. Benny got the best job of all. He took small balls of pizza dough then smacked them as flat as he could. *Smack! Smack! Smack!* Violet placed the rounds of dough onto heated baking sheets. Finally, Jessie spooned Mrs. Piccolo's good tomato sauce over them, along with curls of grated cheese. The pizzas were ready to be baked.

Violet got a good idea, too. She ran downstairs and came back up holding a big white pizza box.

"I don't think we need such a big box for such little pizzas," Benny said. He tried hard not to think about the huge pizzas that usually went into a box that size.

"Oh, yes, we do." Violet disappeared into the bedroom and shut the door.

A few minutes later, wonderful smells began to fill the apartment. The pizzas were nearly ready when the children heard Henry's footsteps on the back stairs. "Mmm," Henry hummed when he came in. "I caught a whiff all the way out at the shed when I put the bike away."

Jessie opened the oven to give Henry — and Benny, of course — a look at the rows of small pizzas just starting to brown at the edges. Henry's mouth watered.

"I just hope those little pizzas work out better than my trip to the gas company," Henry told everyone. "We might need to keep this small oven going a lot longer."

Violet, who had rejoined the others,

looked worried. It wasn't often that her brother set out to fix a problem and failed. "Aren't the repair people coming soon to fix the gas line, Henry? Mr. Piccolo told us that someone had reported the broken gas line a while ago."

Henry shook his head. "That's just it. The gas company said no one had ever called to report it. It's a good thing I checked."

Jessie took a final peek in the oven. The pizzas looked good. But even if they were good, the children couldn't turn out enough of them to get Piccolos' Pizza busy again. They needed that big brick oven in a hurry.

"How soon can the repair people come out, Henry?" Jessie asked.

"They wouldn't say," Henry answered. "We're on the list, but there are several people ahead of us."

"Oh, no!" Violet cried.

"Unless . . ." Henry paused. "Unless I can get someone at Mighty Mufflers to call the gas company right now. After all, the factory is an important business in Silver Falls.

Maybe if the owner calls and says it's an emergency, the repair people will come sooner."

*Ding! Ding!* The timer on the stove sounded. Jessie's pizzas were ready. Everyone gathered around the stove as Jessie carefully slid out two baking trays of small pizzas.

"Oooh, they're nice and hot!" Jessie said. She set down the steaming trays on the enamel kitchen counter.

The pizza plan had worked! While the other children watched, Jessie slid each pizza onto a separate plate. "See? One for each person. I know it's not dinnertime, but let's sample them anyway. If they're good, maybe we can bake another batch for the dinner hour at the restaurant tonight. What do you think?" Jessie asked everyone with a proud smile.

Before Violet sat down at her place she ran to the bedroom again. When she came back she was holding up a big sign she had drawn on the pizza-box cardboard. She held it up for everyone to read:

PICCOLOS' PERSONAL PIZZAS
BIG TASTE IN A LITTLE SIZE
PERFECT FOR DIETERS AND SNACKERS
BUY ONE, GET ONE FREE
FOR A COMPLETE MEAL

"It's fantastic!" Jessie said. "If people could only get a taste of these pizzas, I just know they would start coming back to the restaurant. After we eat, let's ask the Piccolos if we can make up some coupons that say the same thing as the sign. Maybe Henry could go around on the bike and hand them out while we stay here and make more pizzas."

"More pizzas!" Benny called out between bites.

"We may only have a little oven — " Jessie said with a laugh.

"But we have BIG appetites!" Benny cried.

Only Jessie and Violet laughed with Benny. Henry's mind was on something else. How did the gas line get broken, and why couldn't they get it fixed? Well, that was something he was going to find out.

# CHAPTER 4

# The Table in the Corner

In a short time, the back stairs that connected the apartment to the restaurant were busy all day long. Small, unbaked pizzas went upstairs, and hot, steaming ones came back down. Several days after Jessie's Personal Pizza Plan got going, everyone prepared for the lunch hour.

"Try this one," Mrs. Piccolo urged Benny when she set a small pizza in front of him. She knew Benny liked this important job best of all!

The special of the day was Zucchini

Pizza, but Benny looked suspicious. "What are those green things?" he asked Mrs. Piccolo. "They don't look like sausage."

Mrs. Piccolo laughed. "Ah, Benny, some people, they like vegetables better."

"All right." Benny took a tiny bite. "It's pretty good," he said, surprised.

"I thought you'd like it," Mrs. Piccolo said.

Henry came into the restaurant and stamped the snow off his boots. He sniffed the air. "Mmm, nothing like it. I'm out of coupons, so I came back. Boy, it's too bad we're still waiting for the gas line to be fixed. I'd hand out lots more coupons if we could just make more pizzas."

Mr. Piccolo pulled out a chair for Henry and patted him on the shoulder. "Everything's just fine, my boy. We've had more customers in the last few days than in the whole month before you Aldens showed up."

"Have you asked Mighty Mufflers to call the gas company?" Violet wanted to know.

Henry shook his head. "I've tried. But the owner, Mrs. Sturgis, is always away or busy."

Mr. Piccolo smiled proudly at the Aldens. "Now, now. You children eat. Eat this good food. We start in little steps then we take bigger ones. The gas company will come in a few days. Now everybody, dig in."

And so they did. The Aldens and Piccolos tried out several kinds of Personal Pizzas. They each had a special flavor they thought was the best. That's what gave Violet the idea for a pizza contest.

She pulled down the blackboard the Piccolos used to post the menus every day. Across the top, she wrote: *Vote for your Favorite Personal Pizza*. Then she listed all the flavors that Piccolo's offered that day.

"Good for you, Violet," Mrs. Piccolo beamed. "This way we find out which ones our customers like. Then we can make more of them."

The bell on the door jingled. Everyone got up from the table. The Aldens and Piccolos had plenty to do. The lunch hour was about to begin.

For the next two hours, orders were taken. Tables were cleared and reset. The cash register rang over and over again. Benny kept an eye on every table to make sure each customer had plenty of breadsticks.

"Mr. Piccolo," he whispered, when he came back into the kitchen area for more breadsticks, "that lady is here again, the one who's here every day."

Mr. Piccolo peeked through the window on the door between the kitchen and the dining room. "Ah, she was my best customer before things slowed down. But as soon as business picked up, she came right back. She never says too much, but she's a steady one. Always sits at the table closest to the kitchen."

Benny peeked out again. "I think she's doing a crossword puzzle. She eats, then she writes things down. Do you know her name?"

Mr. Piccolo dusted his hands with flour then pushed and pulled on the pizza dough before he answered Benny. "I call her The Lady in the Red Hat."

Now Benny liked this name very much, much better than if the young woman's name were Susan, or Mary, or Ann. "And there's The Man with the Walking Stick."

"And The Woman with the Earmuffs," Mrs. Piccolo joined in. "You see, Benny, some of our customers, they like to talk, and we know their names. But some of the other ones like to come into Piccolos' and just enjoy a quiet meal and read the paper."

"Or do a crossword puzzle," Benny added.

Henry disagreed. "Not a crossword puzzle, Benny. I think she's writing down notes for her job. What's funny, though, is that whenever I go by, she turns the paper over. I guess she doesn't want anyone to see what she's writing."

Soon everyone was much too busy to give any more thought to The Lady in the Red Hat. The lunch hour was nearly over. It was time to clean up then reset the dining room for dinner.

"We'll get the last two checks, Mr. Piccolo," Jessie said. "Then we can get started on tonight's pizzas."

Jessie went over to The Lady in the Red Hat. "Would you like anything else?"

The woman jumped when she heard Jessie's voice. "Uh . . . uh, no, no. Just the bill." The young woman quickly put her notepad and pen into her purse. Then she placed a five-dollar bill on the table without even waiting for her check.

Before Jessie could tell her that five dollars was too much, the woman left. Jessie pushed in the empty chair then gathered up the dishes, crumpled napkin, and the paper placemat.

As she did so, she noticed writing on the placemat: ZUCCHINI PIZZA, 4 VOTES. PEPPERONI, 3 VOTES. PIZZA SUPREME, 5 VOTES.

"What is this?" Jessie asked, puzzled.

"What's what?" Violet wanted to know when she saw Jessie looking closely at the placemat.

Jessie handed the placemat to Violet. "Look at what that customer scribbled down! She copied the votes the customers wrote on the blackboard for their favorite pizzas. Now why would anyone do that?"

Violet was just as puzzled. "Let's show the

Piccolos, Jessie. Maybe they can figure it out."

Mr. Piccolo's full attention was on the pizza dough, not placemats. "A message on a placemat?" he laughed without once taking his eyes or hands off his dough. "Well, that's for you children to figure out. Why last year, a young man wrote a love letter on the back of one of our placemats."

Mrs. Piccolo smiled. "Ah, yes. It was such a beautiful poem."

The children smiled with the Piccolos about the love-letter placemat. But this wasn't a love letter. What was it? The Aldens meant to find out. Jessie carefully folded the placemat and put it in the pocket of her apron.

The children went back to their jobs in the dining room. Benny checked the tables to see that each one had a menu and a full bread-stick supply. He stopped at the table right by the kitchen. "Violet," he called out, "there's a menu missing at this table."

Violet came over. "I'm sure it's here some-where," she told Benny. "The young woman who ate here read her order right off the menu. I'm sure I put it back in the holder. It's got to be there."

Violet and Benny searched under the table and chairs for the missing menu, but it wasn't there.

"Come on, Benny. Let's count up all the menus," Violet suggested. "Maybe the missing one got mixed in with the others. You count half the tables, and I'll count the other half. There should be twenty menus altogether."

" . . . six, seven, eight, nine, ten," Benny counted.

" . . . six, seven, eight, nine," Violet counted at her tables. "They don't add up to twenty. I wonder where that menu went."

The Piccolos told Violet not to worry about the missing menu. But she couldn't help wondering where it had gone. Why would anyone steal a menu?

# CHAPTER 5

# The Lady in the Red Hat Comes Back

Each day brought several new customers to Piccolos' Pizza. The Aldens were sure many more would follow once the restaurant started serving its big pizzas again. Finally the day came when the gas company was going to fix the broken gas line to the Piccolos' brick oven.

Henry could hardly wait for the truck to arrive. "I wonder what's keeping them," he said to the Piccolos. "They were supposed to be here at eight."

By nine o'clock, everyone was beginning

to wonder. After all, Mr. Piccolo had gone ahead and made enough dough to fill most of their large-sized pizza pans. The Aldens had even handed out flyers saying the big pizzas would be back on the menu.

Henry picked up the phone. "I'm going to see what's holding up that truck," Henry said. He dialed the gas company number. "The repair truck was supposed to be here an hour ago," Henry told someone at the other end of the line.

"Canceled!" Henry cried out a minute later. "Of course we didn't cancel. The Piccolos have been waiting over two weeks for the gas line to be repaired."

When Henry hung up, he looked confused and angry. "They said a woman called to cancel the appointment for the repairs. Can you believe it? Anyway, they finally agreed to radio the truck. It should be here in a couple of minutes."

No one was sure what to do next. Mr. Piccolo didn't know whether to divide the big pans of pizza dough into small ones. Mrs. Piccolo wondered if she should put back the extra tomato sauce she had taken out of her deep freezer.

Benny had a breadstick problem. "Should I put these extras back, Jessie?" he asked his sister. "They might get stale if we don't get enough customers."

"No, don't do that," Jessie cried from the front door. She was on the lookout for the repair truck. "They're here! Maybe they can get the big oven fixed before lunchtime."

The children ran out to the truck and waved it down.

"Follow me," Henry told the two workers who climbed out of the truck.

Mr. Piccolo followed them out back, too. Now that the repair people were here, everyone wanted to make sure nothing went wrong.

"Let's make small pizzas, just to be on the safe side," Jessie said. "We can keep an eye on the repairs from the upstairs kitchen. If the brick oven is fixed in time, we'll just roll out some more dough."

The children and Mrs. Piccolo looked out at the backyard. They saw Mr. Irons march out from the factory building to see what was going on. Jessie opened the window so everyone could hear what was happening.

"What are you doing on Mighty Mufflers property?" Mr. Irons asked the workers.

One of workers pulled out a clipboard and held it up for Mr. Irons to see. "We work for the gas company and we're here for repairs."

"Well, all right," Mr. Irons said. "Just stay out of the way of my muffler workers and get off my property as soon as you're done." He turned on his heel and marched back to his office.

A half hour later, one of the repair people shouted up from the backyard. "All set! Your oven should work now."

"None too soon, either," Violet said. "I'll get out more flour and run some warm water. We'll be needing lots more dough this lunchtime."

By the time the noon factory horn sounded, both the apartment oven and the restaurant oven were going full blast. The little restaurant was warm and filled with

good smells. Upstairs, Jessie was in charge of the Personal Pizzas. Downstairs, the rest of the Aldens helped the Piccolos make large-sized pizzas for customers with bigger appetites.

"Something for everyone," Mr. Piccolo said to the Aldens when they came downstairs. "From dieters to hungry folks."

"I'm one of the hungry folks!" Benny joked.

The Piccolos and Aldens barely had time to talk once the lunchtime customers came in. Henry had handed out a huge pile of flyers and coupons that morning. It seemed that every person who got one decided to come in at the same time. There were so many customers, people had to wait for tables. It took a while for Jessie to notice Tom Morgan standing in line right behind The Lady in the Red Hat.

"I guess I'll just have to get a take-out pizza," Tom said when Jessie finally spotted him in the crowd.

She gave Tom a big smile. "Well, we just ordered a good supply of take-out boxes. Big ones and little ones. What size would you like, Tom?"

"Plenty big," Tom answered. "I'm bringing back some lunch for my helpers."

"Helpers," Jessie said, out of breath. "That's what we could use right now. For once, four Aldens aren't enough."

Tom looked around the dining room. "Isn't Nick back yet? I haven't seen him around since he got sick. He must be better by now."

"I wish," Jessie sighed. She handed Tom a take-out menu. "Mrs. Piccolo called him yesterday, but he wouldn't say when he was coming back. If things stay as busy as they are today, we'll definitely need an extra pair of hands around here."

"Not to mention your delivery service," Tom reminded Jessie. "Henry came by the station for bike parts. He said he wanted to build a delivery box on top of the bike so he could take pizzas to people's homes."

Tom pointed to the large Pizza Supreme listed on the take-out menu. "Here's what I'd like. My mouth has been watering for one of these for weeks now," Tom told Jessie. "Well, it looks as if you kids have already made a difference with your good ideas."

Jessie wanted to keep chatting with Tom, but there were onions to be chopped, cheese to be grated, and sausage to be fried. There weren't enough Aldens and Piccolos to get everything done.

"Boy, did that go by fast," Benny said after the last customer had finally left two hours later.

"Everything was a blur, but a nice blur," Violet said with a smile.

She and the other children sat down with the Piccolos to take a welcome break.

Henry checked the restaurant clock. "I guess we'd better get the dining room set up for the dinner crowd."

"You mean we have to do this all over again tonight?" Benny said in amazement.

Everyone laughed so hard, they didn't hear the bell on the front door jingle. When they finally looked up, they saw their steadiest customer, The Lady in the Red Hat, standing in the restaurant.

Only this time, she was The Lady with No Hat. "Excuse me," the young woman called out nervously. "Did I leave my hat here?"

Benny ran to the Lost and Found box under the cash register: "Here it is!" he cried when he held up the woman's red knit hat. "Now you're The Lady in the Red Hat again!"

This made the young woman smile. "I'm also Laurie Baker," she told Benny. "Thank you for finding my hat."

"I wish I could find the menu that was at your table yesterday," Benny said. "It's lost."

The young woman's smile instantly disappeared. She turned to leave.

"Come back," Mrs. Piccolo called out. "Share a cup of tea with us."

The woman looked pale and nervous. She didn't seem too interested in staying.

"Please, Miss Baker," Mrs. Piccolo said. "It's cold out. We'd like to thank you. You're one of the few customers who came to the restaurant in the last few weeks when everything was so slow."

"Sit," Mr. Piccolo insisted, and the young woman finally did.

While Mr. Piccolo got up to put on the kettle, Mrs. Piccolo sat down next to the young woman. "We would have lost our business without people like you who came even when things were not so good."

"I see you're busy now," Laurie Baker said. "Today I even had to wait for a seat."

"Ah, yes, yes," Mr. Piccolo said when he came back with a cup of tea for the woman. "Almost too busy." He nodded at the Aldens. "Of course, we have the best workers in Silver Falls. But even their busy hands and feet won't be enough if we have more hectic days like this one."

Miss Baker seemed to be thinking hard about something. She clinked her teaspoon nervously. "Would you be looking for someone extra to help out?" she asked the Piccolos. "My parents used to have a restaurant before it went out of business. I worked there after school and during the summers. I can cook and wait on tables." Just then she dropped her teaspoon on the floor and bent quickly to pick it up.

The Aldens looked at each other but didn't say anything. They didn't have to; they were all thinking the same thing. None of them could picture this nervous, unsteady person talking to customers or balancing heavy trays.

The Aldens could see that the Piccolos didn't feel any of this. The faces of the couple were full of trust. "Ah, how we could use an experienced person like you in the coming days. After all, the Aldens won't be able to stay forever!" Mrs. Piccolo said.

The Aldens tried to be happy for the Piccolos. They weren't sure about Laurie Baker. But if the Piccolos liked her, then the Aldens would learn to like her too!

CHAPTER 6

# The Mystery Orders

It turned out that Laurie Baker was very good in the kitchen. Thanks to her, the Aldens soon had more free time. But it didn't last long. Henry's delivery business took up a lot of time. Then there were ads to write for the newspaper and more coupons and flyers to persuade new customers to try out Piccolos' Pizza.

Laurie Baker encouraged all the children's plans for going out and getting more business. The Aldens soon found themselves spending more time away from the restaurant than in it.

It was Benny who first noticed how much he missed being around Piccolos'. After handing out discount-pizza coupons downtown one cold morning, he finally complained. "I liked making pizza better than I like selling it."

"I do too," Violet confessed. She was cold and tired from standing on the corner of Main Street. "Right now, I wish I were rolling out circles of nice, warm dough and standing next to the Piccolos' big, toasty oven."

"Me, too," Jessie said.

"Me, three," Henry added as he pushed along his delivery bike on the way back to the restaurant.

Jessie handed Violet her knit scarf. "Here, Violet. You look colder than I am. It does seem funny that we spend more time away from the restaurant now that the Piccolos hired Laurie." Jessie couldn't keep a sad note out of her voice. "I do miss making pizzas," she sighed. "But I guess the Piccolos are lucky Laurie Baker came along. After all, we can only help out for a while. She'll be around a lot longer."

"Maybe it's time to ask Grandfather to come back for us," Violet said in a quiet voice.

No one disagreed.

"Well, let's stick around to see Nick," Henry said. "Mrs. Piccolo said he called and is starting tomorrow."

"I don't think Laurie's going to like that one bit," Benny said. He kicked a piece of ice down the sidewalk. "I bet she wishes she could run Piccolos' all by herself."

The children weren't as eager as usual to get to the restaurant. Since Laurie Baker's arrival, their only jobs were to take orders and clean up.

The Aldens went into the restaurant kitchen the back way. When Jessie stepped inside, she saw rows of small and large pizzas already lined up next to the brick oven. Again, Laurie had done just fine without the children.

At the work counter, Laurie was huddled

over a three-ring binder. She didn't hear the door open. "Need any help?" Jessie asked.

Laurie jumped back and dropped some papers and notes she had been reading. "You . . . uh . . . you're back so soon," she told the children when she saw them standing in the doorway. "I . . . wasn't expecting you for a few more minutes."

Jessie stepped back. Why did Laurie always make the Aldens feel like intruders?

Benny scooted by everyone and began to pick up the papers that had fallen on the floor.

"Never mind those," Laurie said. "Just leave them. There's plenty to do in the dining room. Go!"

Benny felt a lump in his throat. He wasn't used to anyone speaking to him like that. He was only trying to help.

"Okay," the Aldens mumbled as they trooped out.

"Laurie Baker sure is a confusing person," Jessie whispered to Violet and Benny. "Sometimes she likes us, then other times she treats us like pests."

The Piccolos beamed when the children came into the dining room. Mrs. Piccolo pointed to an empty table. "Why don't you children sit down and have some pizza after your hard morning?"

After they'd all eaten, Mrs. Piccolo handed Benny some napkins to fold. Napkin folding wasn't too exciting compared with making pizza from scratch. But Benny did the job anyway.

Violet sat down to help Benny while Jessie and the Piccolos took orders.

"You don't look too happy today, Benny," Violet said.

"Everything was more fun when it was just us helping the Piccolos," Benny whispered. "Laurie's always getting mad at me, like today when I tried to pick up Mrs. Piccolo's recipes."

Violet looked shocked. "That notebook had Mrs. Piccolo's recipes in it? I thought she kept it locked in that old pine cabinet by the sink."

"So did I," Benny said. "But sometimes

Mr. Piccolo forgets to take the key out of the cabinet. Anybody can open it."

"Well, it could be that Mrs. Piccolo gave Laurie the notebook, so she could help make the sauce." Violet sounded doubtful. "And maybe Mrs. Piccolo isn't keeping her recipes secret now that Laurie is her new helper."

"I don't think so," Benny said. "But we'll never find out 'cause she keeps chasing us out of the kitchen!"

There was no time to finish this talk. Violet and Benny got busy making up delivery boxes while Jessie handled the phone orders.

During the busiest part of the lunch hour, something strange happened. The phone rang several times in a row. But each time Jessie greeted the caller, no one answered. After four calls like this, Jessie went over to Mrs. Piccolo.

"Somebody keeps calling but doesn't say anything," Jessie said.

Mrs. Piccolo was too busy to worry. "Maybe it's a wrong number," she told Jessie before disappearing into the kitchen.

The phone rang again. This time Jessie waited for the caller to speak first.

"Hello," a man's voice said. "Is your refrigerator running? Well, you'd better go catch it."

"Oh, for Pete's sake!" Jessie said when she heard this old joke. "I wish whoever is fooling around on the phone wouldn't waste our time during the lunch hour. This is making us lose real orders."

Luckily the fake phone calls stopped. Jessie took down two real phone orders and brought the slips back to the kitchen. She was surprised to see Henry standing there, holding three pizza boxes.

"I thought you were still out, Henry," Jessie said in a concerned voice. "Is something wrong?"

Henry could hardly speak. "This is the third pizza someone ordered. But when I got to the address, no one was there. Three wasted pizzas," he said. "Now they're all cold."

"Oh, no," Jessie said. Like all the Aldens, she hated to waste anything, especially at the restaurant where money was so tight. "Why would someone do this?" she asked.

Before Henry could even take a guess, Violet came into the kitchen looking upset.

"What's the matter now?" Laurie asked when she saw that Violet was about to cry.

"There's a customer out there who left without paying. He ordered a large Pizza Supreme. See." Violet showed Laurie the order she had written down just fifteen minutes before. "He said he ordered a plain pizza. Even though I'm sure he didn't, I told him I'd get him a plain one if he could wait a bit. But he just left without paying! I couldn't bear to tell Mr. and Mrs. Piccolo."

"Maybe you did get the order wrong," Laurie said impatiently. "That's what happened yesterday, too. We can't keep wasting food like this. You'll just have to be more careful. I can't be in two places at once."

Violet swallowed hard. Piccolos' Pizza was busy, and this was no time to cry. Laurie Baker was so cross sometimes. But what made Violet feel worse was knowing for sure she had written down the right order.

Jessie and Henry comforted their sister. Laurie was too busy banging pans around to pay any more attention to Violet.

"It's okay, Violet," Henry said. "At least you just lost one pizza. I lost three of them. The Piccolos can't afford to have these things happen too often. They'll lose their business just when they're getting back on their feet."

No one had the heart to tell the Piccolos what had happened. The children decided they would just be more careful and work harder than ever!

# CHAPTER 7

# Everything Goes Dark

The day began with Mr. Piccolo's cheery whistling downstairs. Upstairs, the Alden children were all asleep, all but Benny, that is. Mr. Piccolo's whistling meant it was time for him to get up.

It was early morning. Benny wanted to get to the kitchen early. That way he could help Mr. and Mrs. Piccolo get the dough started before Laurie Baker got there and scooted him out.

"Tomatoes, potatoes, burritos!" Mr. Piccolo sang out as he took jars and bundles from the big refrigerator. "Pull up a stool, Benny. I need a smart boy like you to measure out some salt, some flour, and some yeast. Do you know what to do?"

"I sure do, Mr. Piccolo," Benny said with a smile.

"Today my old waiter, Nick Marra, comes back. There's nobody to touch Nick when it comes to waiting on tables," Mr. Piccolo said. "Unless it's the Aldens, of course!"

"I can't wait to see Nick," Benny said as he sprinkled yeast over a big bowl of warm water.

A half hour later, Benny noticed Laurie Baker's red hat go by the kitchen window. He jumped off his stool. "You don't have to leave, Benny," Mrs. Piccolo told him.

Benny disappeared upstairs anyway. He knew Laurie would find some way to get him out of the kitchen. He'd rather leave on his own.

It turned out the Aldens weren't the only ones Laurie Baker didn't want near the kitchen. When the children came downstairs later on, the Piccolos were out doing the day's shopping for the restaurant.

Laurie was in charge, and she was arguing with Nick Marra. This surprised the Aldens. They remembered how easygoing Nick was. Nothing ever bothered this young man. No matter how busy the restaurant got, Nick always had a smile for everyone.

But that day, Nick Marra wasn't smiling. His face was red and his bright blue eyes glittered angrily.

"If you hadn't been away so long, the Piccolos wouldn't have put *me* in charge!" Laurie Baker said to Nick.

"Well, they asked me to come back, so I'm . . . ." Nick stopped talking when he saw all four Aldens staring at him.

Jessie went over to Nick first. "Hi, Nick. Remember us? We're visiting the Piccolos and helping them out for a while."

The children were disappointed when they didn't get one of Nick's big smiles or even a friendly greeting. He mumbled a hello and that was it. Violet felt especially hurt that he was so unfriendly.

"Boy, she gets everybody mad, even

Nick," Benny whispered when the children slipped out to the dining room.

For the rest of the morning, the Aldens heard cross words between Nick and Laurie. Nick had his way of doing things, and Laurie had hers. But Violet couldn't help wondering if there was something else bothering Nick.

After lunch, the Piccolos went home to rest. The Aldens were busy with the only job Laurie let them do in the kitchen, washing dishes. Right in front of the children, Nick and Laurie started fighting again.

"It would be easier to box up the take-out pizzas in the kitchen," Nick argued. "They lose heat when you pack them up in the pantry."

"I can't have everyone underfoot when I'm working in the kitchen," Laurie told Nick. "It's bad enough with Mr. and Mrs. Piccolo."

Nick's eyes flashed with anger. "Maybe you don't realize that you're *their* employee, Ms. Baker. They were running this restaurant before you were born."

"And they were losing money until I

showed up to straighten out their business," Laurie said. "Now I don't need you to tell me what to do!"

The Aldens wanted to disappear. Nick Marra actually *did* disappear! He went right out the front door with a loud bang! Jessie, Violet, and Benny finished up their work silently then headed towards the stairs.

"Is the dining room set up for tonight?" Laurie asked before they got away.

The children nodded then shut the door behind them. They didn't come downstairs again until they heard the Piccolos return right before the dinner hour.

"I hope you children aren't coming down with something," Mrs. Piccolo said when she came into the dining room. "I'll make you some spaghetti before we get busy. You all look pale and hungry. My special tomato sauce will fix you right up."

Jessie shook her head. "No thanks, Mrs. Piccolo. We already had something to eat upstairs."

Mrs. Piccolo looked worried. "Something's not right today. I can tell. Nick wasn't himself. Laurie, well, she works too hard. But it's you children I'm worried about. You're too quiet."

"We're okay, Mrs. Piccolo," Jessie told her.

Luckily for the Aldens, some dinner customers came in right then. In a short time, there were so many customers to serve that no one noticed things were not going smoothly at Piccolos' Pizza.

Not once did Laurie look up at any of the Aldens, except when Henry stayed too long in the kitchen waiting for pizzas to deliver.

"Wait in the pantry," Laurie said. "It's too busy in here."

Henry did as he was told. He waited for Laurie to bring the pizzas out to the pantry area. Like Nick, Henry couldn't figure out why they had to box up the take-out pizzas away from the kitchen. But Laurie Baker's mind was made up. The kitchen was pretty much off-limits to Nick and the Aldens.

By six-thirty, every table at Piccolos' Pizza was filled. Mr. Piccolo was just coming out of the kitchen with a large sausage pizza when the lights flickered, then went completely dark. The customers let out an "Ah" at the same time. Only the battery-powered exit lights and the candles on the tables lit the dining room. They cast a soft glow over the nervous diners.

The Aldens heard Mr. Piccolo call out in a calm, sure voice: "Relax, everyone. No problem. Just a little blackout. Just sit tight. I have a couple of flashlights and emergency lamps right here. Nothing to worry about."

Jessie peeked out the restaurant window. She expected to see the whole street in darkness. "It's only the restaurant that lost its power," she told Henry, who had just come back from his deliveries.

"I know. Everything went black just as I came in the kitchen," Henry said.

"Where's Laurie?" Jessie asked. "Does she have any light in there?"

"You know, that's the strange thing," Henry said. "The lights went out just as I got here, but Laurie already had a flashlight in her hand when she came up the cellar stairs."

Even in the dim light Henry could see his sister's eyes widen. "Why would she need a flashlight down in the cellar unless she knew the power was going to go off?"

"Just what I was thinking," Henry answered. "But you know what she said? That she heard a noise down there and grabbed a flashlight so she could go and check on it. Then she tried to blame everything on Nick."

"Nick? I'm pretty sure he was out here when the power went off." Jessie looked over toward the kitchen and saw Nick setting up the emergency lights. "You know, Henry, now I'm not so sure. We were so busy, I don't really know where he was."

The customers grew restless. They wanted to go home.

"Listen, everyone," Mr. Piccolo called out. "My helpers here, they're going to wrap up your pizzas for you to take home. It's take-out night for everyone. Nobody pays."

A few people clapped. The Aldens couldn't clap. They knew this emergency was going to cost the Piccolos a lot of money.

Mr. Piccolo went on. "On your way out, my good friend Benny Alden here will give you a coupon for free pizza when you come back to the restaurant. All right?"

"All right!" a few adventurous customers cheered.

Nick came out with a stack of pizza boxes. Laurie handed everyone a spatula. Then they all went around to each table boxing up the unfinished pizzas. As promised, Benny handed out free pizza coupons.

Mr. Piccolo sighed when the last person left. "What a night! We'll have to get an electrician out here first thing in the morning to see what the problem is," he said.

"Or *who* the problem is," Laurie muttered under her breath after the Piccolos went into the kitchen.

In the low light, the children saw Nick glare at Laurie, but he said nothing. Shortly afterwards he left the restaurant with barely a good night.

When Mrs. Piccolo came out of the kitchen, Violet noticed she was crying softly. "What is it?" Violet asked.

Mrs. Piccolo took Violet's hand and led her to the big white deep freezer. "My sauces. They will thaw out without electricity. The tomatoes are from our garden last summer. Special tomatoes for Piccolos' sauce. We will lose more than money if we lose these frozen sauces."

Laurie Baker was the only one of the tired group who didn't seem upset by this. "Well," Laurie said, almost cheerfully, "you can teach *me* how to make some new batches. We don't even need electricity for that. We can start tomorrow."

Mrs. Piccolo smiled at the young woman. "Ah, such a willing worker you are. But there are no fresh tomatoes at this time of year. The sauce would never be the same."

Before Laurie had an answer for that, Violet came up with a solution. "Benny, Jessie, Henry. Go get your jackets, boots, and hats and follow me."

"Where are you going?" Laurie Baker asked suspiciously. "Nothing's open at this hour. You'll never find anyone with a freezer for all the frozen sauces and meats in here."

It was too dark for Laurie to see Violet's ear-to-ear grin. "Oh, yes, we will!" she shouted before she went outside ahead of her brothers and sister.

Violet handed everyone a shovel. "Now dig as much snow as you can."

"I get it!" Benny said after the first shovelful. "We're not looking for a freezer, we're making one! Just like we made a refrigerator in a brook when we lived in the boxcar."

"That's right, Benny," Violet cried. "Only now it's a freezer, not a refrigerator. And we're using snow, not a brook."

Henry held up his shovel like a flagpole. "Let's hear it for Violet! Hip hip hooray! Hip hip hooray!"

The Aldens cheered and shoveled as fast as they could to make their "outdoor freezer" for Mrs. Piccolo. They couldn't see that Laurie Baker was watching them from the kitchen window and that she didn't look at all happy with what the Aldens were doing.

# CHAPTER 8

# A Surprise Confession

The next morning, the sun was shining, and so was every light at Piccolos' Pizza. The children ran outside to see how their "freezer in the snow" was working. The Piccolos were already packing up the frozen meats and sauces to bring inside.

"When did the power come back on?" Jessie asked.

"This morning at six," Mr. Piccolo answered. "I came out early to cover your little freezer before the sun came out. When I arrived, the electricity was back on. The emergency people from the light company said a truck from the muffler company backed into the pole last night. This knocked out the electricity for a while. Now it's all fixed."

Henry and Jessie walked back to the shed to get some carrying crates.

"I'm glad the power is back on," Jessie said. "I guess we were wrong to think that Laurie or Nick caused the blackout."

Henry nodded. "Still, I can't figure out why Laurie didn't seem upset. She almost seemed glad to have to make the new sauces."

When Henry and Jessie came back with the crates, they saw Laurie Baker coming up the driveway.

"I see everything was saved," Laurie said without a smile. She only stopped frowning when she saw the Piccolos.

"Good morning, Laurie," Mr. Piccolo cried. "I guess you know that Violet here rescued everything last night. My homemade sausages, Nina's tomato sauces, everything is still frozen solid."

"So I see," Laurie said before she went inside.

Mr. Piccolo brought in the last of the freezer containers. "Well, now that everything is set for the day, Nina and I can go out for the morning shopping," Mr. Piccolo told the children.

Mrs. Piccolo reached for the marketing basket she kept by the freezer. "With these children and Laurie and Nick working together, we could take the whole day off!"

But Mrs. Piccolo was wrong about everyone working together that day. The minute the Piccolos left, the phone rang in the dining room. When Jessie answered it, Nick told her he wasn't going to be in.

"Who was that?" Laurie asked when Jessie hung up.

"Nick," Jessie answered in a puzzled voice. "He can't come in today. He didn't say why."

"Fine," Laurie said. "It's easier without him underfoot. Now I need all of you to hand out these flyers in town for today's special. You don't need to come back until eleven."

The children knew what Laurie expected them to do. They put on their warm clothes and took the stack of flyers. When they went past the muffler factory, they handed out a few flyers to some of the workers going into the building.

Jessie tried to hand one young man a flyer, but he went by too fast. "Here, try our . . . Nick!" Jessie suddenly cried. "What are you doing here?"

Nick pulled down his hat and pulled up his scarf to cover his face before he disappeared into the building.

"Are you sure that was Nick?" Violet asked. "Why didn't he answer you?"

"I'd know those blue eyes anywhere," Jessie said. "I wonder if he's started a job here. Maybe that's why he didn't come to the restaurant today."

The children spent the rest of the morning trying to puzzle out what was going on with their old friend.

By ten-thirty, the Aldens were out of flyers. They didn't want to upset Laurie by coming back too early, so they walked slowly.

"Something is still bothering me about last night," Jessie said when she saw a Mighty Mufflers delivery truck go by. "Why was Laurie the only one who wasn't upset?"

"She almost seemed glad that it happened because then she could help the Piccolos make more sauce," Henry said.

"There's so much work in the restaurant already, why would she want to make those sauces?" Violet asked. "That's a lot of work."

Benny shuffled along with his hands in his pockets. "And I bet she wouldn't let us help. Or Nick either!"

"Nick is the other part of this puzzle," Jessie said. "At first I thought he was acting strange because of Laurie. But he moved out of the apartment and stopped coming to Piccolos' before she even started working there."

"What if," Henry began, "what if Mighty Mufflers hired Nick because he *did* work for the restaurant and knows all about it? If the factory wants to put Piccolos' out of business for some reason, they could use Nick to hurt the restaurant."

"No!" Violet broke in. "Nick would never

help anyone harm the Piccolos. I just know he wouldn't."

The other children knew how much Violet liked Nick. She knew him better than any of the other children. He would never cause problems for the Piccolos. Violet was sure of that.

When the children finally reached the restaurant, there was a new problem to figure out. A truck from the county health department was parked in the driveway of the restaurant.

"What's the health inspector doing here?" Violet asked.

"He goes around to restaurants and food stores to check that everything is neat and clean," Jessie said.

"I know the dishes are neat and clean," Benny said proudly.

The children weren't a bit worried about the health inspector. They knew Piccolos' Pizza was the cleanest restaurant in Silver Falls.

The Aldens heard a man's loud voice coming from the kitchen. "Now take out every pot and pan! And all the canisters of flour, too! This freezer needs to be five degrees colder, so you'll have to throw out what's in there."

"But, but," Mrs. Piccolo began, "the freezer will be the right temperature in a few minutes. We lost our electricity last night and . . ."

"Your electrical problems are not my problems." The man checked off something on his clipboard. "Everything in that freezer has to be thrown out!"

Henry wasn't going to let this happen. "Sir, this food has been packed in ice all night. I think if you just open a few containers, you'll see that everything is frozen colder than your requirements. As Mrs. Piccolo said, the freezer is nearly at the right level now. Please, could you check?"

"Hmph!" the inspector said. "I'll check, but if it's a tenth of a degree off, out this food goes. Understand?"

Henry nodded.

The man pulled the tops off several con-

tainers of tomato sauce. "All right," the man muttered. "Now please run through the steps you follow to store your food and prepare your pizzas."

Mr. and Mrs. Piccolo explained how they made their dough and grated their cheese fresh every day. Mrs. Piccolo showed off the gleaming jars of tomatoes she put up at the end of every summer from her garden full of tomatoes. She pointed to the pots of herbs sunning themselves on the kitchen windowsill.

As the inspector checked over and under the cabinets, the Piccolos explained everything from how far ahead they made their sauces to how long they let their pizza dough rise. By this time, the inspector had calmed down. He even looked a little hungry!

All this talk didn't interest Benny much. He went out to the dining room. He was surprised to see Laurie Baker sitting at her usual table, right by the kitchen. She seemed to be listening in on the conversation coming from the kitchen, then writing things down in her notebook.

Before Laurie even saw Benny, he went back to get Jessie.

Right after the inspector left, Jessie came out to the dining room. "What are you writing down, Laurie?"

The young woman was so startled she slammed her notebook shut and dropped her pen. "Nothing — nothing important," she answered. "Isn't there something you two should be doing besides spying on people?"

"We weren't spying," Benny said. "I just came out to do my jobs." As Laurie handed Benny the silverware tray, he brushed against her notebook. A piece of paper that was sticking out floated to the floor.

Jessie picked up the paper and read it out loud. "Two tablespoons of olive oil. Six cloves of garlic. Two jars of tomatoes. Four teaspoons of bay leaves."

"It's four teaspoons of *basil*," Mrs. Piccolo said when she came into the dining room. "Not bay leaves. Why are you reading my recipe for tomato sauce, Jessie?"

Jessie stared at Laurie. "It was in Laurie's notebook," she said, puzzled.

Laurie took the paper from Jessie. "I didn't. It's . . . it's something else."

"May I see that, Laurie?" Mrs. Piccolo asked softly.

"It's . . . I had a reason," Laurie said when she finally handed Mrs. Piccolo the piece of paper.

Mrs. Piccolo looked hurt and confused. "Why? Why did you write this down? What are you hiding from us?"

Laurie sank back into her chair. Her voice trembled. "I needed the recipe for your sauce, Mrs. Piccolo."

Mrs. Piccolo put her hand on Laurie's shoulder. "My recipe? Why would you need such a thing?"

Laurie didn't look up when she answered. "I wanted to help my parents reopen their restaurant in Maytown. It went out of business last year. I thought if they knew how to make your good pizza and how to run a restaurant like yours, they could make a go of it."

"So you came to get experience here?" Mr. Piccolo said in a hurt voice. "Why didn't you tell us when you started coming here for lunch? We would have offered you a job. Why have you lied to us?"

Laurie looked up and tried to explain. "I was afraid you wouldn't hire me if you knew my parents had a restaurant, so I waited until you really needed someone. I know that was a terrible thing to do. I realize that, now that it's too late."

Everyone was silent.

Finally, Mr. Piccolo took a deep breath and spoke to Laurie. "If you had told us the truth, we would have taught you all our business. We're not worried about a restaurant all the way out in Maytown competing with us! You didn't have to sneak around trying to figure out Nina's recipes."

Mrs. Piccolo took Laurie's hand. "My recipes are not a secret. That is just our joke."

"I'm so sorry for the way I acted. You trusted me so much, and I didn't deserve it," Laurie said, looking up at Benny. "I'm sorry for the way I treated these wonderful children. I was afraid they would find out what I was doing."

"You were trying to help your parents," Mrs. Piccolo said. "I can understand that."

"They only have one more month on their lease," Laurie said. "I thought if I could re-open their restaurant in time, I would make enough money so they could sign a new lease."

The Piccolos and Aldens listened closely as Laurie explained.

"Every time I came in to eat I took a few notes," Laurie went on. "There was so much to remember — the contest Violet thought up, the new menu, all the dishes you needed. I took a menu home with me and peeked into the kitchen a few times when I sat at this table."

"Were you the person at the window the first day we got here?" Benny asked.

"I was," Laurie confessed. "I knew you were all in the dining room, so I tried to get a good look at the layout of the kitchen. But after your dog started barking, I left."

"What about the fake orders?" Henry asked.

"And that man who said he ordered a plain

pizza then left without paying?" Violet added.

Laurie shook her head. "I had nothing to do with those mix-ups. Please believe me." She looked at the Piccolos. "I'm not sure I've been the only one sneaking around the restaurant. A few times when I came by after hours, I noticed a man watching the restaurant, too. I never saw his face. I don't know if he's the one who left without paying or the one who called in fake orders." Laurie stopped then lowered her voice. "Maybe it's someone you know already."

"Now, now, no one would harm us," Mrs. Piccolo said in her trusting way. "These are problems anybody could have."

"What about getting the broken gas line fixed?" Henry asked. "The gas company said it was a woman who canceled the repair truck."

Laurie paused. "I had nothing to do with the broken gas line or the blackout last night. I was down in the cellar getting more supplies. I did see that you might lose the sauces. Then Mrs. Piccolo could have taught me how to make new batches." Laurie looked up at Violet. "After Violet came up with the outdoor freezer idea, I thought of another way to find out about the secret sauce."

Laurie stopped talking. She looked scared. "I was the one who called the health inspector."

The Aldens and Piccolos felt as if Laurie had thrown ice water on them.

"It's not what you think," Laurie said quickly. "See, I knew the health inspector, at least I knew the one who used to stop by my parents' place. I figured you wouldn't have any problems since Piccolos' is so clean all the time. I just wanted to find out everything about how you run the restaurant and make your sauces and sausages. I had no idea the new health inspector would be so mean. I'm most ashamed of that," Laurie said, sniffling. "I feel so terrible."

The Aldens felt terrible, too. The Piccolos were so generous and good. What Laurie had done was very wrong.

"I'll just go," Laurie said sadly. "I've caused you enough trouble."

"Now, now, now," Mr. Piccolo said. "You don't get away that easy, young lady. No, no. We have a plan, don't we, Nina?"

Mrs. Piccolo looked as surprised as everyone else. Then Mr. Piccolo whispered something in her ear. She nodded her head.

"Yes, that's a fine idea." Mrs. Piccolo turned to Laurie. "If you're willing to work free for the next few weeks, we will teach you all we can about running a pizza restaurant. What do you think about that?"

Laurie's answer was to give a huge hug to both Piccolos. "I think I'm a lucky person. I'll make up for everything, I promise. Thank you for giving me a chance."

"Well, miss, your lessons start right now," Mr. Piccolo joked. "So get out your notebook."

"What are you doing, Benny?" Laurie asked when he sat down with a pencil and paper.

"I'm going to Piccolos' Pizza School, too!" he answered.

# CHAPTER 9

# Turned Away

The restaurant was so busy that the Piccolos and the Aldens soon forgot their troubles with Laurie. Everyone worked side by side in the kitchen and dining room now. Benny taught Laurie his way of smacking down the dough nice and flat. Mrs. Piccolo helped her start some herb seedlings to take to her parents' restaurant.

Mr. Piccolo came huffing and puffing into the kitchen after one busy lunch hour ended. It was tiring for him to go back and forth between the kitchen and dining room. "If only Nick were back, then my pizza family would be complete," he said. "We could use his strong arms to carry these trays. Ah, well, I suppose even young fellows can get sick."

"Young fellows *can* get sick," Jessie whispered to Henry after Mr. Piccolo went back to the dining room, "but that's not what's wrong with Nick."

Henry took off his coat now that the lunch deliveries were over. "I just saw Nick again going in the factory gate, but he pretended not to see me."

"Maybe Nick isn't sick the way Mr. Piccolo thinks," Violet said. "I'm just sure something's wrong that he can't tell us about right now."

"Like what happened to you, Laurie," Benny said as he grated piles of cheese. "What if he wants to open a restaurant, too?"

Henry patted Benny's head. "Not likely. What I can't understand is why he just doesn't come straight out and tell us he's working at the factory. The Piccolos would be disappointed, but they'd understand."

"He's probably all caught up in his own troubles," Laurie said. "I saw him, too, when I left work last night, but he went right by. He's always wrapped up in a hat and scarf so we won't recognize him. I still wonder if he's the man I saw around the restaurant the first few weeks I started coming here."

The children spent a quiet afternoon starting to pack. Grandfather Alden was picking them up in just a few days.

"I want to see Grandfather and Watch," Jessie said as she folded some of her clothes, "but I wish things would go better here before we drive back to Greenfield."

"I know what you mean," Henry said quietly. "I was counting on Nick to be here next week when Tom's son starts delivering pizzas. He's going to need someone to supervise him for a while. Everyone else is so busy."

"If Nick would only let us talk to him," Violet said. "Maybe he'll come by this afternoon before the restaurant opens for dinner."

But Nick did not return that afternoon. When the children came down to the restaurant at four-thirty, the Piccolos looked upset.

"Nick, he just called in sick again," Mrs. Piccolo said. "I'm getting so worried about him. He never really got better. These young people don't always take good care of themselves."

Laurie and the Aldens looked at each other then looked away. The Piccolos were always so trusting.

When Mr. Piccolo brought over the lunch checks and money from the cash register, everyone was relieved. Each afternoon the children sat with the Piccolos to match the lunch money and lunch checks before dinner. This job took a lot of careful attention. There wasn't any time to talk about Nick.

Mr. Piccolo put down the drawer of money at the center of one of the big restaurant tables. "Here, Benny. You and Violet can wrap the coins in wrappers for the bank."

Jessie and Henry, who were both good in math, got busy adding up all the check totals. Then everyone compared the lunch checks with the lunch money. Every day the numbers came out even.

They had finished counting just before five when the front door bell jingled, then jingled again and again. This surprised everyone since most dinner customers arrived after five-thirty. In just a few minutes, five or six children stood in the dining room. All of them were waving bright yellow coupons.

"We came for the free sodas," a boy about Violet's age said when he came over to the table. "And pizza, of course. We've got our own money for that!"

The Piccolos, the Aldens, and Laurie had no idea what this boy was talking about.

Henry took the boy's coupon and read it out loud: "BUY A SLICE OF PIZZA, GET A SODA FREE. THIS COUPON GOOD BETWEEN 5:00 AND 7:00 ONLY. FOR CHILDREN, AGES TWELVE AND UNDER."

Mr. Piccolo looked over Henry's shoulder then took the coupon. "Is this one of the coupons you handed out today?" he asked the Aldens in an alarmed voice. "I can make pizza, but free sodas would cost us all the profit we made at lunch. And to give away something during the dinner hour — there won't be room for our regular customers who pay for a whole meal."

Jessie studied the yellow coupon too. "This isn't the coupon we handed out. Ours was for a ten percent discount on lunch pizza."

The boy looked upset. "Somebody left a stack of these on a table in the gym lobby. That's where I got it." The boy held up some coins. "See, I do have money for the pizza."

By this time, a man in a sweatsuit had come over to find out what was going on. "Is there a problem here? I'm the director of the day program at the Silver Falls middle school. We have a sports program there during the winter vacation. These kids here have been playing hard all day, so your coupons seemed like a great idea."

The man had barely finished talking when another crowd of children came into the restaurant. Each of them had a free soda coupon, too!

"I'll seat them," Laurie said, "then we'll figure out what to do."

"There's nothing to do but feed these

hungry children," Mrs. Piccolo said.

In the kitchen, the Piccolos pulled out more sauce from the deep freezer. Benny got busy grating more cheese. Henry and Jessie headed down to the cellar to bring up cases of soda.

"This is going to cost the Piccolos a fortune, Henry," Jessie said.

Henry looked upset. "I can't believe some one would go to all this trouble to make up coupons. They look like the ones we gave out, but they say something totally different. If a lot of kids keep coming in with these coupons, the Piccolos could lose their business."

Henry's worse fears came true when he and Jessie came upstairs and checked the dining room. "Oh, no! Every table is filled with kids. Do they all have coupons?"

Mr. Piccolo sighed. "Every one, I'm afraid. Another bunch came in and said there was a stack of coupons at the ice-skating rink too. Every child in Silver Falls who wasn't at the gym was at the skating rink!"

Violet went over to some regular customers who were talking to Mrs. Piccolo.

"Sorry, Mrs. Piccolo," one woman was saying. "Thanks for the offer of take-out pizza. But my husband and I were planning on eating out. We'll come back another night when it's not so busy."

"Wait, wait!" Mrs. Piccolo said. "Here. Take one of our discount coupons. I'll cross out 'lunch' and write in 'dinner' on it. You get a discount on any pizza you order the next time you come in for dinner. Okay?"

Violet couldn't even hear what the couple answered. The restaurant was noisy with the laughter and shouts of children. During the next two hours, the Piccolos turned away dozens of customers while Silver Falls kids of all ages enjoyed pizza slices and free sodas during the busiest night of the week.

As Violet headed into the kitchen with some orders, she saw a familiar face in the front window of the restaurant. It was Nick, peeking in. Violet waved for him to come in. She went to the door. If Nick was feeling better, Piccolos' Pizza could sure use him right then. But by the time Violet got to the door, Nick had disappeared.

Violet didn't tell anyone about Nick. When she came into the kitchen, she could see how tired the Piccolos were. They had enough trouble already. They didn't need to find out that Nick wasn't really sick.

Mrs. Piccolo put on her glasses and read the order Violet handed her. "Another pizza. I'll get this one ready." While she worked, Mrs. Piccolo wondered whether someone really was trying to hurt their business. "Why? Why would anyone do such a thing? And to get children involved! I can't believe this could happen," she muttered.

By the time the last child left after seven o'clock, the restaurant had gone through six cases of soda. The Aldens rinsed all the cans and put them in the recycling barrel.

After everything was cleaned up, Laurie and the Aldens shooed the Piccolos out the door. "Time to go home and rest," Laurie told them. "We can take care of things and close up."

Jessie turned off the neon sign in the window and locked the front door. "Come on, Henry. I want to go over to the factory and see if they had anything to do with this. Do you want to come too, Violet?" she asked her sister.

Violet stared out at the front porch of the restaurant. It almost seemed as if she could see Nick's face still looking in.

"What's the matter, Violet?" Henry asked when he saw her standing so still. "You look as if you just saw a ghost."

Violet shook her head sadly. "Not a ghost, Henry. About an hour ago when I was taking an order, I saw Nick looking through the window. But when I went out to talk to him, he was gone."

Jessie didn't want to believe this. "Are you sure, Violet? There were so many people going in and out. We had to turn some old customers away. Maybe one of them looked inside and decided not to come in."

Violet wanted to believe this too, but she couldn't. The face in the window *was* Nick's. Had he been the one to hand out the coupons? Had he come by to see if this terrible plan had worked? Violet shivered. Then she put on her jacket. She wanted to go to the factory with Henry and Jessie. Maybe they would find out something that would explain what was going on with Nick.

"We'll be back in a while," Jessie told Laurie and Benny as they stacked up dishes next to the sink.

When Jessie, Violet, and Henry reached the front gate of the factory, Henry said: "It's almost time for the night shift to come in. Maybe we can blend in with the crowd then look around for Nick."

But Henry didn't need to go inside the factory to find Nick. Just as the children reached the front gate, they spotted the young man. He wasn't alone. He was walking out of the building with a young woman and someone else. As they got closer, the children recognized the third person — Mr. Irons, the factory manager.

The Aldens stepped away from the streetlight into the shadows of the parking lot so they wouldn't be spotted. Mr. Irons, Nick, and the young woman headed toward Mr. Irons' fancy car.

"I have to go out and check on a few things," Mr. Irons told Nick and the woman. "I'll drop you both off. Don't keep my secretary out too late. She has to be at work first thing tomorrow morning."

Even in the dark, the Aldens could see that Nick and the young woman didn't look too happy when they heard this. But they got in the car with Mr. Irons anyway.

The children didn't say anything. After Mr. Irons drove off, they walked back to the restaurant slowly. Seeing Nick with Mr. Irons upset them more than anything else that had happened.

Finally Violet spoke up. "I guess I was wrong about Nick. Maybe Nick isn't just working on mufflers. Maybe Mr. Irons hired him because he knows all about Piccolos' Pizza."

"There's *one* thing about Piccolos' Pizza he doesn't know," said Jessie. "But I have an idea about how we can fix that."

# CHAPTER 10

## *Surprises for Everyone*

"Sorry, Henry, don't take your jacket off," Laurie said when Henry came through the back door of the restaurant the next day at lunchtime. "Jessie just gave me one more delivery order. It's for a Pizza Supreme."

"I know all about it," Henry said with a smile. "It's a surprise delivery."

Laurie was puzzled. "What do you mean?"

"What Henry means is that we have a new plan," Jessie told Laurie. "We've been trying to get Mr. Irons on the phone, but he won't talk to us. Today, we're going to deliver a pizza right to his office."

Laurie couldn't help laughing. These Aldens just never gave up!

Benny sniffed at the big pizza box. "Mmm. We think Mr. Irons doesn't know how good this pizza is. If he is the one who's trying to hurt Piccolos', maybe he'll stop once he knows he can get this good pizza every day if he wants!"

"If he gets one bite of this," Violet said, "he'll be glad, not mad, that Piccolos' is right next door."

Jessie headed toward the apartment upstairs. "I'm just going to make sure he's in his office. I can sometimes see him from the apartment window."

When Jessie bounded back down into the kitchen, she cried: "Everything's a-okay. Let's go!"

The children were out the door before Laurie could stop them. They were sure their plan was going to work.

"Okay, ready everyone?" Henry said when they reached the factory gate. "Now let's just stroll in like all these other people."

The four friendly, polite children had no trouble getting into the building.

"Pizza delivery for Mr. Irons," Jessie said to the woman at the front desk.

"Hmm, I guess Mr. Irons is getting tired of deli sandwiches," the woman said with a smile. "Sixth floor, then down the hall to the right. His secretary is out now, but I'll let him know his lunch is here."

The children hadn't counted on anyone telling Mr. Irons he was getting a pizza. They crossed their fingers.

"Mr. Irons, your lunch is on its way up," the woman said. Luckily for the Aldens she didn't say what that lunch was going to be!

The children stepped into the elevator with several other people. They noticed some of them sniffing the good pizza smell.

"I just had lunch," one nice business-woman told Jessie, who was carrying the Pizza Supreme. "But I must say that pizza you have there smells mighty good."

"It *is* good," Benny said. "It's from Piccolos' Pizza right down the street. Here's one of our flyers."

"I'll be sure to get over there soon," the woman said. She gave all the children a big smile. "Or maybe you can deliver one right to me next time!"

"Just call," Benny cried when he and the children reached the sixth floor.

"Whew, I was a little worried there," Jessie said. "After all, Mr. Irons told Henry over the phone that Mighty Mufflers wouldn't accept any deliveries from Piccolos'."

Henry laughed. "He'll have to accept this. It's free."

The children went down the hall. They were a bit nervous but not *too* nervous. After all, how could anyone, even Mr. Irons, resist Piccolos' Pizza Supreme?

"Here's his office," Violet said before she opened the door. "His secretary still isn't back, so I guess we should just go in."

The children approached the door that said: MAXWELL IRONS, MANAGER. They nearly dropped the pizza when they heard a loud crackling noise. It was the intercom on the secretary's desk.

A voice boomed out: "Ms. Donella! Call the deli and find out what on earth happened to my lunch. A man could starve in here waiting for them to deliver it!"

Benny knocked on the door and pushed it open when he heard Mr. Irons say: "Come in, for heavens sakes, come in!"

"Here's your lunch," Benny piped up.

"Whaaat!" Mr. Irons yelled. "What are you doing here? And where's my turkey sandwich?"

The children were too busy to answer his question. Jessie whisked out a placemat and put it in front of Mr. Irons along with a knife, fork, and a big checked napkin from the restaurant. Meanwhile, Violet and Henry expertly cut a huge steaming slice of pizza and placed it on a large white plate.

"Just what is going on here?" Mr. Irons bellowed. He yelled into his intercom: "Ms. Donella, Ms. Donella, who let these kids in here?"

No one answered at the other end. The

man tried not to sniff the delicious warm smell of tomato, dough, and mozzarella cheese.

"I told my secretary I wanted a turkey sandwich. She can't even get a simple lunch order straight," Mr. Irons said.

It was clear that Mr. Irons was hungry. But it was also clear that he was very angry and was not going to cut into the big slice on his plate. Jessie took the pizza cutter and cut a much smaller piece. She lifted it onto a paper napkin and handed it to Mr. Irons so fast he couldn't refuse it.

When he opened his mouth to say something, Jessie said: "Take a bite. Go ahead."

Without thinking, that's just what Maxwell Irons did. Then he took a second bite and a third.

"Isn't it good?" Violet said.

"Isn't it the best pizza you ever had?" Benny added.

Mr. Irons was too busy tasting, chewing, and swallowing to say anything, which gave Henry a chance to speak first. "Mr. Irons, you don't seem to know it, but you have the

best pizza place in Silver Falls right next door. Why do you want to hurt their business?"

Mr. Irons stopped eating. Angrily, he pointed a finger at the Aldens. "Now you kids listen to me! That tumbledown place has caused me nothing but headaches. I want that space for a factory cafeteria. The factory is busier than ever, and I can't have my people running over there for pizza! Understand? Now tell that Mr. Whatever-His-Name-Is that I'm going to make him an offer to buy that place or else he's going to have even more than a broken gas line or a black-out or a bunch of kids wanting a cheap meal."

"So it *was* you!" Jessie said.

"The Piccolos have owned that restaurant for over thirty years," Violet said sadly. "It was busy until you got here."

"Why couldn't you have just talked to the Piccolos?" Henry asked Mr. Irons. "You could have worked together."

"Work with a couple of pizza bakers who should be retired?" Mr. Irons said in a cruel voice. "I want a company cafeteria on that spot, and I'm going to get it no matter what other stunts I have to pull."

The children moved to gather up the pizza and dishes when they saw a woman standing in the doorway.

"It's the lady I gave a flyer to," Benny whispered to Jessie.

"Uh, I'm sorry about these kids, Mrs. Sturgis," Mr. Irons said as he grabbed for his phone. "I'll call Security to get them out of here."

The woman stepped forward. "You will do nothing of the kind, Mr. Irons. I over-heard everything you told these children over the intercom on Ms. Donella's desk."

"Uh . . . oh . . . well, these kids sneaked in here without permission."

"Only because they wanted to help out some people who have done business in Silver Falls for many years," Mrs. Sturgis said. "I am horrified by the way you have managed my business while I was away. You certainly did not have my permission to harm my neighbors. You are fired!"

Mr. Irons glared at the children. "You,

you nosy kids. I knew you were trouble the day I saw you at the gas station."

"That's quite enough, Mr. Irons," Mrs. Sturgis said. "You can come back for your things after hours. I do not wish to see you again."

On his way out the door, Mr. Irons nearly ran down a young woman who was coming into the outer office.

"Mr. Irons," the young woman said. "Are you leaving?"

"For good, Ms. Donella," Mrs. Sturgis said. "Perhaps you can work as my secretary now that I'm back at the office."

The young woman blushed. The Aldens knew they had seen her before.

"Are you a friend of Nick Marra's?" Violet asked.

The young woman looked down. "Why, yes, I am," she said. "He should be here any minute. We went out to get Mr. Irons his lunch."

"So Nick does work for Mr. Irons?" Violet asked.

"Oh no," the young woman answered.

"You see, Nick and I are engaged to be married. He comes by for me at lunch. Sometimes Mr. Irons makes me run errands on my lunch hour, so Nick helps me out."

Right then, Nick Marra appeared in the doorway. He was holding a large brown bag from the deli. He looked completely confused when he saw Mrs. Sturgis, Ms. Donella, and all the Aldens standing there.

"How do you do, Nick?" Mrs. Sturgis said, as she put out her hand to him. "I'm Lydia Sturgis, the owner of Mighty Mufflers. I don't think Mr. Irons will be needing that lunch today since he just ate an excellent pizza."

Nick shook his head. "What's going on? Why are all of you here?"

Violet spoke up. "We came here to see who was trying to hurt Piccolos' Pizza. And we just found out why we saw you around the factory so much," Violet said with a huge smile. "Ms. Donella told us everything. Now we know it wasn't you causing problems at the restaurant, but Mr. Irons."

Nick looked terrible. "I had to leave the

restaurant. I saw how Mr. Irons felt about Piccolos', and I was afraid he'd fire Marie — Ms. Donella — if he knew I worked at Piccolos'. And I was afraid that if the Piccolos found out I was engaged to Mr. Irons's secretary, they'd think *I* was against them, too."

Mrs. Sturgis took Nick's hand. "Well, I may have to fire Ms. Donella if you *don't* go back and work there! My employees need a good restaurant nearby, and I plan to send a lot of business over to Piccolos', starting today. They are going to need a strong young man like you."

The children waved out the window of Grandfather Alden's car. "Good-bye Mrs. Piccolo! Good-bye Mr. Piccolo! 'Bye Laurie! 'Bye Nick!" they called out as Mr. Alden pulled away.

As they passed the huge Mighty Mufflers billboard, the children could see a half dozen work people moving the big sign to the side. Slowly, the Piccolos' Pizza sign painted on the side of the building came into view.

"Next time, we'll find it on our first try," Henry said.

Benny sniffed the air. "I guess I've been around pizzas too much lately. I can still smell pizza."

"You sure can," Jessie laughed. "When we made the Pizza Supreme for Grandfather, Violet and I made an extra one for Tom. We're going to deliver it when we stop by for gas."

"Oh, goody," Benny cried. "Then I can try out the gumball machine one last time."

Tom was already out by the gas pumps when Mr. Alden drove up. He gave everyone a wave. "Thanks for bringing me lunch," he told the Aldens. "My mouth's been watering for the last half hour just thinking about this Pizza Supreme," Tom said with a laugh. "So Benny, tell me something. Did you finally have a big adventure?"

"I'll tell you in a minute," Benny answered before he ran into the station.

He went straight to the gumball machine and ran his hands over it. "Abracadabra, bibbledeebee, send a prize gumball just for me."

He put in one of the pennies Mrs. Piccolo had let him keep after redeeming the soda cans. He turned the crank then closed his eyes. When he opened them, he picked up a silver gumball. He couldn't believe it.

"Hey, I won!" he yelled to Tom and the Aldens. "I won a silver gumball on the first try!"

Tom gave him a friendly punch on the shoulder. "Good for you, Benny. Now what can I get you as a treat?"

Benny laughed. "This special gumball is my treat. I'm going to save it as a souvenir of this trip. I'll trade it in next time we come for pizza in Silver Falls!"

GERTRUDE CHANDLER WARNER discovered when she was teaching that many readers who like an exciting story could find no books that were both easy and fun to read. She decided to try to meet this need, and her first book, *The Boxcar Children*, quickly proved she had succeeded.

Miss Warner drew on her own experiences to write each mystery. As a child she spent hours watching trains go by on the tracks opposite her family home. She often dreamed about what it would be like to set up housekeeping in a caboose or freight car — the situation the Alden children find themselves in.

When Miss Warner received requests for more adventures involving Henry, Jessie, Violet, and Benny Alden, she began additional stories. In each, she chose a special setting and introduced unusual or eccentric characters who liked the unpredictable.

While the mystery element is central to each of Miss Warner's books, she never thought of them as strictly juvenile mysteries. She liked to stress the Aldens' independence and resourcefulness and their solid New England devotion to using up and making do. The Aldens go about most of their adventures with as little adult supervision as possible — something else that delights young readers.

Miss Warner lived in Putnam, Connecticut, until her death in 1979. During her lifetime, she received hundreds of letters from girls and boys telling her how much they liked her books.